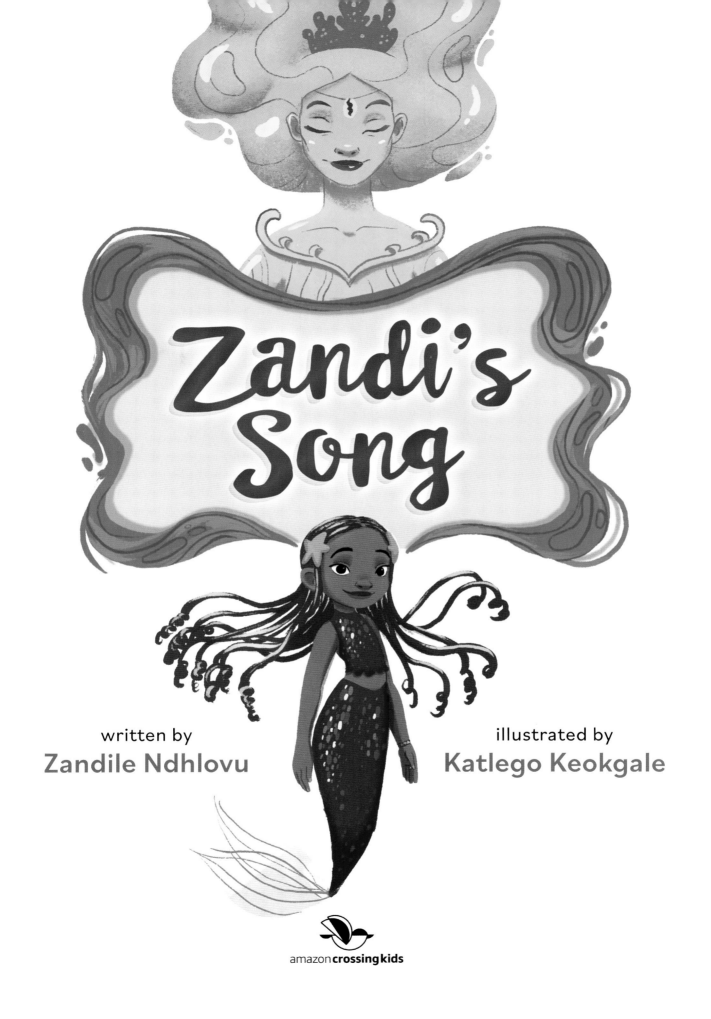

Zandi's Song

written by
Zandile Ndhlovu

illustrated by
Katlego Keokgale

amazon crossing kids

Previously published as *Zandi's Song* by Pan Macmillan South Africa in South Africa in 2023.
First published in English by Amazon Crossing Kids in collaboration with Amazon Crossing in 2024.

Published by Amazon Crossing Kids, New York, in collaboration with Amazon Crossing

www.apub.com

Amazon, Amazon Crossing, and all related logos are trademarks of Amazon.com, Inc., or its affiliates.

ISBN-13: 9781662520105 (hardcover)
ISBN-13: 9781662519840 (eBook)

The illustrations were rendered in digital media.

Book design by Tanya Ross-Hughes
Printed in China

First Edition
10 9 8 7 6 5 4 3 2 1

Resources for Ocean Conservation

- **Kids Conservation Zone—Project AWARE:** diveagainstdebris.org/publication/kids-conservation-zone

- **National Geographic Kids—Save Our Oceans!:** natgeokids.com/uk/home-is-good/save-the-ocean/

- **National Oceanic and Atmospheric Administration—For Kids:** oceanservice.noaa.gov/kids/

- **World Ocean Day for Schools:** worldoceanday.school/

Author's Note

This book was inspired by my own experiences with the ocean. Like many Black South Africans, I didn't learn to swim as a child. And I didn't live near the ocean. But at age twenty-eight, I went on a snorkeling trip that changed my life. I had never seen anything that looked so beautiful: all these weird and wonderful animals coexisting together in peace at the bottom of the ocean. I immediately felt at home.

From that day on, my goal was to make the ocean a place that everyone can enjoy. In 2020, I became my country's first Black female free diving instructor. I have since launched the Black Mermaid Foundation to inspire the next generation of divers and encourage people of color to learn to swim.

But the ocean that I love so much is in danger from pollution. For our future generations to be able to enjoy it, we need to do everything we can to protect it—just like Zandi in this book! I hope you will join Zandi in protecting our seas.

Zandi was always thinking about the ocean.
At night, she would dream about big waves
rushing toward her, pulling her to lands unknown.

During the day, she could hear it whispering, telling her
that it was time . . . that it had always been waiting for her.

"Your life is here," it said. "This is your home."

Zandi was scared at first. She wasn't a strong swimmer.
Would she be safe?

"The moment you touch me, you'll know that
I will not harm you," the ocean promised.

Zandi dipped her feet into the water and . . . was met
by colorful fish and an ocean floor that looked
like it was lit from underneath
by the brightest lights.

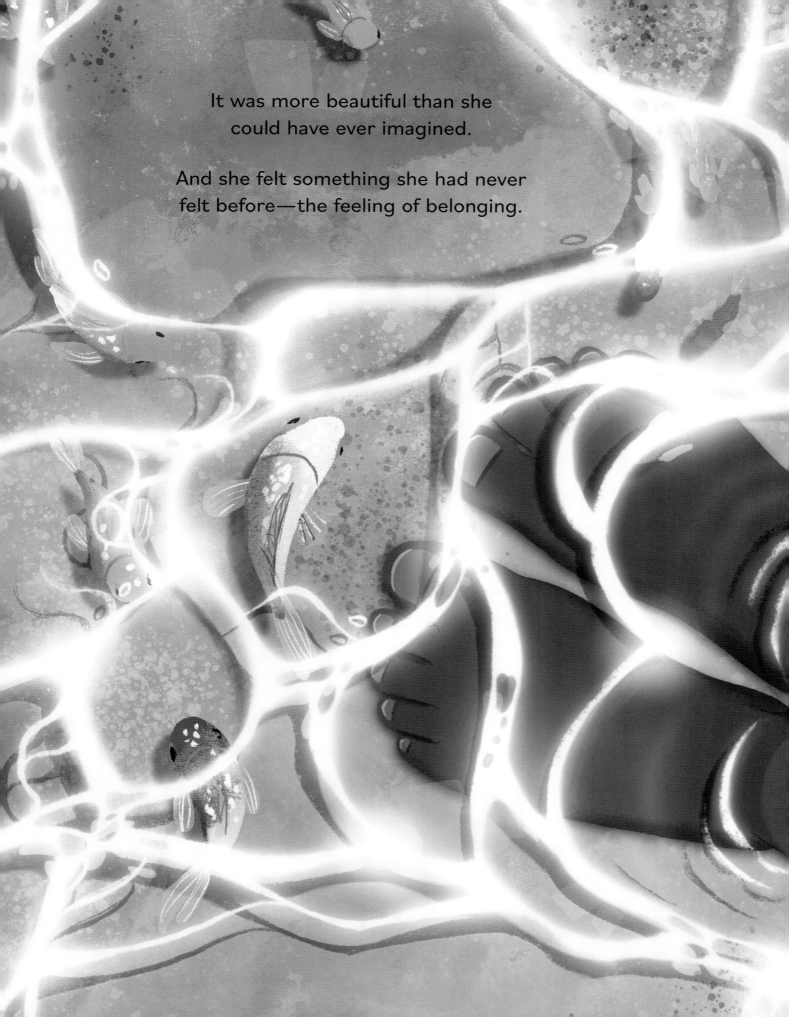

It was more beautiful than she
could have ever imagined.

And she felt something she had never
felt before—the feeling of belonging.

"To make it easier for you to swim," the ocean said,
swirling gently around her, "I will offer you a gift."

A small sandstorm built up around Zandi.
She felt her legs tingling. Glittery scales started forming,
from her toes right up to her belly button,
with a shimmering top to match.

"Thank you!" she said. Zandi slowly slipped
deeper into the water.

But the ocean wasn't done. Zandi's Afro was turning into braids.
She couldn't believe her eyes! It reminded her of her grandmother
and all the other women in her family.

"There is one more thing . . . ," the ocean said.
She placed a beaded bracelet in Zandi's hand.
"This is a reminder of your lineage, in the water and
on land. When you miss your home on land, tap your
bracelet twice, and it will transport you back."

Zandi carefully fastened the bracelet
around her wrist.

"You can call me Maya," said the ocean.
"I have waited for you for a very long time."

Zandi was surprised. "Why were you
waiting for me?" she asked.

"Do you remember the story your grandmother told you?"
Maya asked. "The one about the man who warned
the villagers to stop throwing garbage into the river, because
the water mother and her children were struggling to breathe?"

"Yes," Zandi replied. "Gogo knows many stories . . . That story reminded
me not to litter, and to tell everyone else about the problem too."

"Your gogo passed this story on to you, Zandi, and you will tell it
many times because you have been chosen to protect me."

Zandi shook her head. "But I'm just a child," she said. "How will I be able to help you?"

"I will show you all the wonders inside me," Maya said as she swept Zandi up in her arms. "And soon, you will realize that you are not separate from anything else in this world.

"We are all one. Everything in the universe speaks.
Maybe not in words, but if you listen closely,
you will hear exactly what it is saying. You will learn
to understand the song of the ocean."

As the current swept Zandi along,
she noticed trash everywhere.

"Where does all of this come from, Maya?" she asked.

"Most of the trash is carried out to sea by streams and rivers. The plastic can stay here for thousands of years. Sea animals can become entangled in it or eat it, causing injury and even death." Maya looked very sad.

"This is why I need your help."

They were moving so fast now that Zandi could barely
see anything. Water and light and the shapes of sea creatures
passed by them in a whirl.

"Here we are at last," Maya said as they
started to slow down.

"I have brought you to a very special place.
It is called kwaUmkhomazi."

Zandi saw a big bridge with turbulent
brown water flowing under it.

"There used to be many whales in this area," Maya explained. "And each year, the villagers would celebrate the coming of the whales with drums and dancing. The whales knew they were safe here to nurse their young."

In her imagination, Zandi could see the whales with their babies, feeling safe and loved in the waters that they had traveled so far to reach.

"The whales also took care of the people," Maya continued. "When there was a drought and the people suffered from hunger, the whales would gather and make a sacrifice. One of the oldest whales would beach itself so that the village would have food for months to come. The villagers had a strong relationship with the whales, and so each year the whales' numbers grew."

Zandi looked around her in wonder. Could there really have been a time when humans and whales had such a strong bond?

"And dolphins, Maya?" she asked.
"Did the dolphins come here too?"

"Yes. The dolphins warned the villagers that danger was approaching. Strangers from faraway places arrived and began to build very close to the sea's edge. This forced the villagers farther inland. The strangers had weapons, and the villagers couldn't stop them. But worst of all, they used their weapons to kill the whales. Thousands of whales lost their lives, and the villagers still mourn for them. The whales also come to these shores every year and mourn the family members they lost."

By now, Zandi was crying.

"I know it hurts to hear this, my child,"
Maya said, "but you must know and
remember the history of this place,
so that you can make sure
it never happens again."

Just then, a whale appeared. Zandi looked at it in awe.
She had never seen anything so big in her life.
The whale blew out strongly through its blowhole.
Zandi swam up to the whale, closed her eyes,
and pressed her hand against its skin. It felt as if
they had met before, perhaps in a dream.

The whale started singing, vibrating into Zandi's
ears and heart. Zandi couldn't make out the words
of the song, but she knew that it was beautiful.

Then she dived deep into the blue,
where at last she could hear the whale's song.

"Welcome to our home. This has been our home for thousands of years. We have seen the most beautiful things but have also experienced hard times. We have known of your coming for a long, long time, and we welcome you. You have a big task ahead of you. So we come to bring you blessings and wish you well along this journey.

"From the deepest sea to the surface, whenever you need us,
simply call, 'Uthandiwe, uthandiwe, uthandiweeeee!'
And we will rise to meet you."

"Thank you for trusting me," Zandi said.
"I will do everything I can to protect you."

The whale looked at Zandi kindly.
"Travel safely, dear friend. We will meet again."

As Zandi waved goodbye to the whale, she suddenly realized
how tired she was. It had been a long day, but she had become
stronger. She smiled when she remembered the whale's song.
Uthandiwe is a powerful word. It meant that she was loved.
It was a word that would call on all the creatures of the ocean
when she needed them.

"We have come to the end of our journey for now," Maya said.
"You must rest. I have shown you many things, but it is the people
on land who need you most. Tell them what you have seen,
and do all that is necessary to protect the ocean.
Remember: wherever you are, you can find the water,
and I will be there."

Zandi was sad to leave Maya, but she was also missing her people on land. She tapped her bracelet twice and almost immediately found herself back at home. She sang softly to herself as she made her way through the streets of the city.

"The seas are alive.
The waters are alive.
From the smallest fish
to the biggest whale.
It is all alive.
It is all alive."

Zandi went out and spread her song and all she had learned
as far and as wide as she could.

From then on, after days of sharing her song,
Zandi dreamed of big beautiful whales.
She dreamed of a smiling moon and shooting stars.
But she also saw herself—she was beaming from the inside.

She was finally **home**.